An Intergalactic Gypsy's Guide to the Universe

By Olivia Choi

Olivia Choi

An Intergalactic Gypsy's Guide to the Universe

Copyright © 2019 by Olivia Choi

Self-published

intergalacticgypsy523@gmail.com

FOR THE SANITY

OF HUMANITY

I.

Hello my friend
My name is Olivia
I don't follow trends
Or standard criteria

I am a transient millennial
Seeking a higher vibration
Learning is perennial
Stimulated by exploration

I am an intergalactic gypsy
Exploring a new planet
A galaxy-hopping hippie
Always discovering in transit

II.

They say I'm spontaneous
I should slow down
Empowering the miscellaneous
Never seen with a frown

Living life in extremes
To validate our existence
Dreams don't stay dreams
When pursued with persistence

III.

We are powerful, flowerful leaders
Planting smile and laughter seeds
Inspiring lovingly disruptive connection
Creating kind and open abundancy

Let's make humans smile each day
To stimulate intellectual conversation
Let love, passion and kindness light the way
Along with the constellations

IV.

Going down the rabbit hole
Taking off the masks and layers
Authenticity is the goal
Achieved with visionary team players

One defense mechanism appears
Followed by another
Illuminating all our fears
As we flee from society's smother

V.

No plans have been made
Nor will they be
Submitting to the flow
Where will it take me?

Submitting to the process
Embarking on unknowns
Unsure of any progress
Pushed out of comfort zones

I keep asking myself
What's waiting for me there?
If I find out
Maybe I'll share...

VI.

Life doesn't have to be so hard
You don't always have to think
Do what's easy, don't bombard
And everything will be in sync

Play with a sense of urgency
Moving key pieces every day
Acting as a source for convergency
Creating the silly game we play!

VII.

I am here to give you strength
To ask you the hard questions
I am here to hold safe space
And illuminate your blessings

I request you step into courage
And consciously choose to look
It is your time to flourish
You will be my guidebook

VIII.

What is your vision?
What do you want to do?
What is your mission?
How do you act as source to make it true?

Are you playing team?
What are your results?
Have you invited people into your dream?
Or retreated to comfort on impulse?

Do you act from fear?
Or live in abundance?
Do you hide behind your career?
Or live in our oneness?

IX.

What kind of person are you?
Do you always say YES?!
What energy do you accrue?
Do you push others to the test?

Do you live a life of no regrets?
Do you always do your best?
Are you living your life with no upsets?
Are you grateful for this life quest?

X.

I am committed to create and hold space
To give open awareness a debut
Shifting the perspective of a familiar place
For you and me to break through

Stepping into vulnerability
To wipe the slate of the past
Enjoying a collective humility
To create tranquility that lasts

XI.

I am playing the game
And making every rule
I invite you to do the same
Knowing you have all the tools

You can make anything happen
I know you already do
I invite you to step back and tap in
To recognize and control the zoo

XII.

Are you ready to build?
And maneuver the field
What makes you thrilled?
What has yet to be revealed?

XIII.

I will only hold you high
I will not hold you small
All I ask is that you try
And get back up when you fall

I am here to watch you fly
It is time to lift off
Let out a great sigh
It is time to blast off!

XIV.

You have all the answers
I act as a trigger
I sit back and observe the dancers
Holding space for your rigor

Who are you being?
What gifts do you hold?
What are you not seeing?
Are you playing small or being bold?

XV.

Take space
Don't hold back
This is a safe place
To put your life on track

Course correct if necessary
It is easy to wander
Create knowing you are a visionary
I invite you to ponder

XVI.

What is your vision?
Does your life align?
What is your mission?
Do you understand that now is the time?

How do you play?
Are you on the sidelines or in the game?
What are you creating today?
Are you playing big or acting tame?

What are your rules?
How can I understand?
Do you set boundaries as tools?
Can I peek into your wonderland?

XVII.

I invite you to dream
What is your perfect life?
One where there are no screams
A place with no agony or strife

What do you really want?
What else is possible?
What do you want to flaunt?
Are you willing to be accountable?

XVIII.

I invite you step into possibility
And picture your perfect world
Knowing this is your responsibility
I look forward to watching it unfurl

Be grateful for what you've got
And flaunt what you want
Make reality of your thoughts
Knowing you are your greatest confidant

XIX.

Are you playing it safe?
Are you acting from comfort?
Are you giving yourself space?
And creating a buffer?

What are you resisting?
Don't you know you are great!
What habits are persisting?
Do you still hesitate?

XX.

I invite you to look
And be clear in your stand
Author your life book
Don't be shy, MAKE IT GRAND!

Know you are the origin
You are the life force
We are connected by oxygen
Guiding Earth's course

XXI.

You are powerful
You have arrived
Do you paint the world flowerful?
Or live only to survive?

Are you a sheep?
Or are you a leader?
Are you asleep?
Or are you a seeder?

Do you listen with intention?
Or do you always talk?
Are you coming to create intervention?
Or do you hold space to remove blocks?

XXII.

I am here to listen
I am here to support you
I am on a world mission
Inviting you to break through

Break through the barriers
Break through your mind
Break through and be merrier
Break through and redesign

This is a constant process
There will be no end
We are in exponential progress
Are you ready to transcend?

XXIII.

This is a call to action
A human transaction
A pinnacle of inaction
Of near-extinct reactions

Let's gain some traction
Let's commit to reclaim
Let's start a chain reaction
Let's never refrain

XXIV.

I am not my feedback
I am not my results
I will not give you flack
I am here to consult

I am because you are
I ask you to think about that
We are creators at large
And that is a fact

I am and you are
You are and I am
We are connected from afar
We are connected by the microgram

XXV.

Our visions create our reality
Our perceptions create our truth
Grounded in personal actuality
How do we maintain our youth?

XXVI.

Is your faith in humans restored?
Is your sapien perspective renewed?
There is no time to be bored
I am me, him, she and you

Do you choose a new life?
A path where anything goes?
A community without strife?
People who keep you on your toes?

Do you live life in extremes?
To validate our existence?
Or do you keep your dreams as dreams?
Scared to step into persistence…

XXVII.

Are we a connected identity?
Through serendipitous curation?
Are we one living entity?
With an unknown duration?

Parallel to the undertow
Away from where we swam
Are you ready to let go
To be who I am?

XXVIII.

I am superfluous
Inspiring your dreams
Never accepting acts that are treasonous
Always committed to playing team

Let's sit in dreams for a minute
What are your deepest desires?
Are you present and in it?
What lights your internal fire?

If you could not fail
What would you do?
What would your life entail?
What OuTrAgEoUs things would ensue?

XXIX.

If you don't ask
It is most certainly a NO
What a silly task
Contemplating to and fro

XXX.

I am shifting toward serenity
To enhance my transformation
Embracing my identity
No longer in a place of hesitation

Feeling empowered to live
Supported and terrified too
I am on this Earth to give
That is all I know to be true

XXXI.

Why are you smiling?
Life isn't always fun
What memories are you compiling?
When you're always on the run

XXXII.

I live in possibility
Coming from abundance
Stepping into responsibility
Recognizing everything is wondrous

Do you live in possibility?
Do you come from abundance?
Do you step into accountability?
And recognize what's wondrous?

XXXIII.

I request you take a look
At how you play the game
Are you happy with your book?
Or are you continuing to do the same?

I request you step into urgency
Knowing your importance
Assuming a role in the convergency
Knowing your impact is enormous!

XXXIV.

I am open to receiving
Seeking out my guides
Coming from a place of believing
And understanding from all sides

Guides approach me in my dreams
They flow through me in my words
They hold me to extremes
And support me to fly high with the birds

XXXV.

We are all light
We are all from the stars
We all shine bright
And we have all been to Mars

It is time to remember
There is no need to fret
The awakening of all members
Is a question of yet

It is happening exponentially
We are experiencing a shift
We are urgently stepping into eventually
Recognizing our gift

XXXVI.

We bring the gift of life
And we spread our roots
We get to break through this strife
And celebrate our fruits

We created this world
Do you live in the world you want to see?
Has your vision unfurled?
Are you who you want to be?

We are here to create
We are here to love
We are here to awake
And be the peace dove

We are here to enjoy
We are here to be present
We are here to employ
And live in contentment

XXXVII.

There is no need to be happier
Than being content
No need to be more and snappier
We get to be and invent

There is no need for more or less
We get to be who we are
We are on this planet to do our best
As other entities watch from afar

XXXVIII.

Our spiritual guides are by our sides
We close them off as they continue to steer
They will not allow you to push them aside
Metaphysical guides will always be near

Our guides speak through different vectors
They resonate with what we understand
They are the ultimate human respecters
Helping us realize what was planned

XXXIX.

We are here to support our wins
We are here to enjoy
We show up with a silly grin
And call out all the decoys

We are here for spiritual healing
Connecting by abolishing "I" and "my"
We are here to share the same feelings
Thinking in "we," "ours," and "cry"

XL.

Knowing we are we
And we are one
Then we get to be
Playing this game and having fun!

We get to play big
We don't get to play small
We are dancing a fast jig
Holding each other tall

We choose a new life
A path where anything goes
A community without strife
A family that ebbs and flows

XLI.

How can you do it all?
What else is possible?
Are you following a call?
Are you unstoppable?

With freedom comes choice
And a shift is inevitable
You have now found your voice
And the results are incredible

When lack, fear and anger disappear
Abundance, love and gratitude arise
Smiles and laughter persevere
And the whole world comes alive!

XLII.

The time is NOW!
We ARE source for it all!
The results are WOW
We are no longer playing small

We are stepping into urgency
Exercising our responsibility
Grateful for the convergency
As we step into possibility

XLIII.

There is no path
The path is now
There is no aftermath
You may ask how?

All shall reveal itself in time
Continue to trust the flow
Keep shifting your life paradigm
And sharing the afterglow

XLIV.

Don't be scared
You came looking for answers
You are getting what you declared
Along with life dancers

XLV.

Our bodies are a reflection of Earth
Our heart is the center and fiery core
We all had a collective birth
Let's step back and stop keeping score.

We are mostly water
We, are one
Observe Earth like it's your daughter
And thrive on the sun

We are reflections of each other
The o-zone is our aura
Depleting as we recognize one another
Patching with beautiful flora

XLVI.

We are planting seeds
To fertilize growth
Inspiring all dreams
To create lasting hope

XLVII.

The artichoke field inspires glee
As we embrace individuality
Each flower stands alone in the community
The purple field represents human unity

XLVIII.

Do we need a cleanse?
A great purification?
Surrounded by friends
And no justification

XLIX.

The mind is neutral
Until a story is attached
The story is rarely truthful
Yet we regard it as fact

Let down our walls
Let other people in
Slow down to a crawl
And see what happens

L.

We are not from here
We are from the stars
We are all sightseers
Visiting from afar

We hit an immense roadblock
We are uninspired by the sites
We are on a cultural journey
Running away from the lights

We are observing the patterns
Because we already know
Trying to remember Saturn
And letting the manifestation flow

LI.

We are newest to the galaxy
And our thoughts are interspersed
Limited by our physicality
Unknowingly guided by the universe

Adventures of the intergalactic gypsy
Will always go on
There is no time to be tipsy
It is a new dawn

LII.

We keep asking ourselves
What's waiting for us there?
If we find out
Maybe we'll share…

We seek to find triggers
To unlock knowledge inside
Recognizing humans as mirrors
And every person as our guide

LIII.

We are a collective guru
And I am because you are
I am grateful for all that you do
Thank you for being my star

LIV.

We landed eons ago
And created a society
Adapted to the flow
And imposed our insobriety

We shift and change this planet
We don't ask for permission
We treat it like it won't vanish
We have a crazy addiction

LV.

We are quick to follow the pack
Even when our gut tells us it's not right
We are scared of being attacked
Being ridiculed and in fright

Why don't we stand for our vision?
Who really wants war?
Let's create an aligned mission
And stop keeping score

There is more than enough for us all
If we step back and choose to live
We do not get to let each other fall
When we choose to continuously give

LVI.

Connecting our identity
Through serendipitous curation
We are one living entity
With an unknown duration

Our faith in humans is restored
Sapien perspective renewed
There is no time to be bored
I am me, him, she and you.

Oh what a strange long trip it has been…

www.ingramcontent.com/pod-product-compliance
Lightning Source LLC
Chambersburg PA
CBHW070400120726
47909CB00008B/2932